M000074258

# Love *from* Pooh

x

*To*..............................

*With love from*

..............................

Love
from
Pooh
×

A. A. Milne
Illustrations by E. H. Shepard

EGMONT

Hand in hand
we come
Christopher Robin and I
To lay this book in your lap.
Say you're surprised?
Say you like it?

$S$ay it's just what you wanted?
Because it's yours –
Because we
**love**
you.

A. A. Milne

# The Food of Love

'The only reason for
making honey is so
as *I* can eat it.'

# Love, Sweet Love

'It all comes, I suppose,'
he decided, 'it all comes
of *liking* honey
so much.'

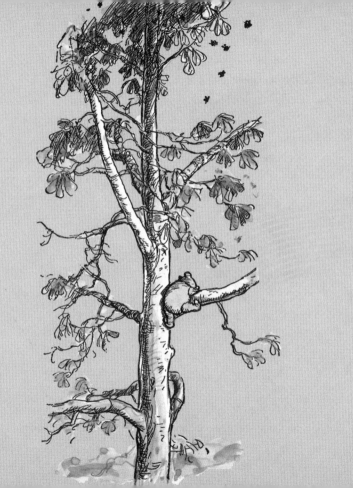

# *Falling in Love*

CRACK! 'Oh help!' said Pooh, as he
dropped ten feet on to the branch
below him. 'If only I hadn't—'
he said, as he bounced
twenty feet on to the
next branch.

# Frustrated
# Love

He could see the honey,
he could smell the honey,
but he couldn't quite
reach the honey.

# Love's Duty

'Then would you read a
Sustaining Book, such as
would help and comfort a
Wedged Bear in Great
Tightness?'

# *Enduring Love*

Christopher Robin looked
after him lovingly,
and said to himself,
'Silly old Bear!'

# Love's Luck

Pooh thought how nice it would
be if they met Christopher Robin
suddenly but quite accidentally,
and only because he liked
Christopher Robin
so much.

# *Love*
# *Speaks*

'I have been Foolish and Deluded,' said he,
'and I am a Bear of No Brain at All.'

'You're the Best Bear in All the World,'
said Christopher Robin soothingly.

'Am I?' said
Pooh hopefully.

# *Helpful Love*

'Eeyore,' Pooh said solemnly,
'I, Winnie-the-Pooh,
will find your tail for you.'

'Thank you, Pooh,' answered
Eeyore. 'You're a real friend.'

# *Lovesick*

But he couldn't sleep.
The more he tried to sleep,
the more he couldn't . . .
Every Heffalump that he counted
was making straight for a
pot of Pooh's honey,
*and eating it all.*

# Love
## One Another

'Oh, Bear!' said Christopher Robin.
'How I do love you!'
'So do I,' said Pooh.

# Loving
## and Giving

'Stay there!' he called to Eeyore, as
he turned and hurried back home
as quick as he could; for he felt
that he must get poor Eeyore
a present of *some* sort
at once.

# *Love*
## *is*
# *Constant*

Wherever I am
there's always Pooh,
There's always Pooh
and me.

Whatever I do, he wants to do,
'Where are you going today?' says Pooh:
'Well, that's very odd 'cos I was too.'

# *Love Token*

'It's for Pooh.
The best bear in all the world.'
'Oh!' said Pooh.
'Oh, Pooh!' said everybody
else except Eeyore.

'Thank you,'
growled Pooh.

# The Hour
## of
## Love

'Nearly eleven o'clock,'
said Pooh happily.
'You're just in time for a
little smackeral of
something.'

*Love*
*at*
*First Sight*

'Worraworraworraworraworra!'

Pooh got out of bed and
opened his front door…
'Oh!' said Pooh.

'Hallo!'
'Hallo!'
'I'm Pooh,' said Pooh.
'I'm Tigger,' said Tigger.

# Cupboard Love

He found a small tin of
condensed milk . . . so he took it
into a corner by itself, and
went with it to see that
nobody interrupted it.

# Love Affair

Pooh said good-bye affectionately
to his fourteen pots of honey,
and hoped they
were fifteen.

'Fourteen,' said Pooh.
'Fourteen. Or was
it fifteen?
Bother.'

# Love Song

Oh, I like his way of talking,
Yes, I do.
It's the nicest way of talking
Just for two.

# Lessons
## of Love

'There's a thing called
Twy-stymes,' he said.
'Christopher Robin tried
to teach it to me once,
but it didn't.'

# The Power of Love

'There are twelve pots
of honey in my cupboard,
and they've been calling
to me for hours.'

Piglet sidled up to
Pooh from behind.

# Love
## -in-a-Mist

'Pooh!' he whispered.

'Yes, Piglet?'

'Nothing,' said Piglet, taking
Pooh's paw, 'I just wanted
to be sure of you.'

# Lovelorn

'Oh, there you are,' said
Christopher Robin carelessly,
trying to pretend that he
hadn't been anxious.

'Here we are,'
said Pooh.

'Let's go and see
*everybody*,' said Pooh.

# Love Needs No Excuse

'We'll go because it's Thursday,'
he said, 'and we'll go to
wish everybody a Very
Happy Thursday.'

# *Loving*
## *Thoughts*

Pooh thought that being with
Christopher Robin was a very
good thing to do, and having
Piglet near was a very
friendly thing
to have...

# Love of Learning

Pooh, with his back against one of the
sixty-something trees, and his paws
folded in front of him, thought
how wonderful it would be
to have a Real Brain
which could tell
you things.

# In the
# Name of
# Love

And he took a stick and touched
Pooh on the shoulder, and said,
'Rise, Sir Pooh de Bear, most
faithful of all my Knights.'

Love Letters

# True Love

'Oh, Pooh!' cried Christopher
Robin. 'Where *are* you?'
'Here I am,' said a growly
voice behind him.
They rushed into each
other's arms.

# Love
## Forever

'Pooh, promise you won't
forget about me, ever.'

'I promise,' said Pooh.

First published in Great Britain 2002 by Egmont Books Limited
This edition published in 2015 by Egmont UK Limited
The Yellow Building, 1 Nicholas Road, London W11 4AN

ISBN 978 1 4052 7615 3

Printed in Malaysia

MIX
Paper
FSC FSC® C018306